HUMPHREY SAYS . . . READ THIS BEFORE YOU BEGIN!

	1	2	3	4	5	6	7	8	9	10	11	12
1	1	2	3	4	5	6	7	8	9	10	11	12
2	2	4	6	8	10	12	14	16	18	20	22	24
3	3	6	9	12	15	18	21	24	27	30	33	36
4	4	8	12	16	20	24	28	32	36	40	44	48
5	5	10	15	20	25	30	35	40	45	50	55	60
6	6	12	18	24	30	36	42	48	54	60	66	72
7	7	14	21	28	35	42	49	56	63	70	77	84
8	8	16	24	32	40	48	56	64	72	80	88	96
9	9	18	27	36	45	54	63	72	81	90	99	108
10	10	20	30	40	50	60	70	80	90	100	110	120
11	11	22	33	44	55	66	77	88	99	110	121	132
12	12	24	36	48	60	72	84	96	108	120	132	144

Each number is illustrated by a group of differently colored animals. The multiplication table for each number is presented on the page opposite the number, and the numbers are color-keyed throughout.

A simple game of counting groups of animals can be played on the right-hand pages—a first step in understanding tables! On the page for the number 5, for example:

1. First count all the dogs up to 25.

2. Count the dogs in groups of 5. Every 5th dog is colored to emphasize the groups, *but counting must be from left to right and from top to bottom of the page.* Thus, 5 groups of 5 dogs is 25 dogs, or 2 groups of 5 dogs is 10 dogs, and so on.

3. Use the multiplication table at the foot of the page to check your answers by color matching. The answer square to 5 × 5 shows number 25 and is pale pink—the same color as the 25th dog! Similarly, the answer square to 2 × 5 shows number 10 and is dark yellow— the same color as the 10th dog, and so on.

4. Play this times-table game on any page by counting the animals and checking your answers.

Children will enjoy counting the animals as they gather around Humphrey the Horse.

Library of Congress Cataloging in Publication Data

Peppé, Rodney.
  Humphrey the number horse.
  SUMMARY: A simple introduction to numbers and the principles of multiplication.
  1. Numeration—Juvenile literature. 2. Multiplication—Juvenile literature. [1. Numbers. 2. Multiplication] I. Title.
QA141.3.P46   513'.2   77–18782

ISBN 0–670–38666–9

HUMPHREY THE NUMBER HORSE

Fun with Counting and Multiplication

Rodney Peppé

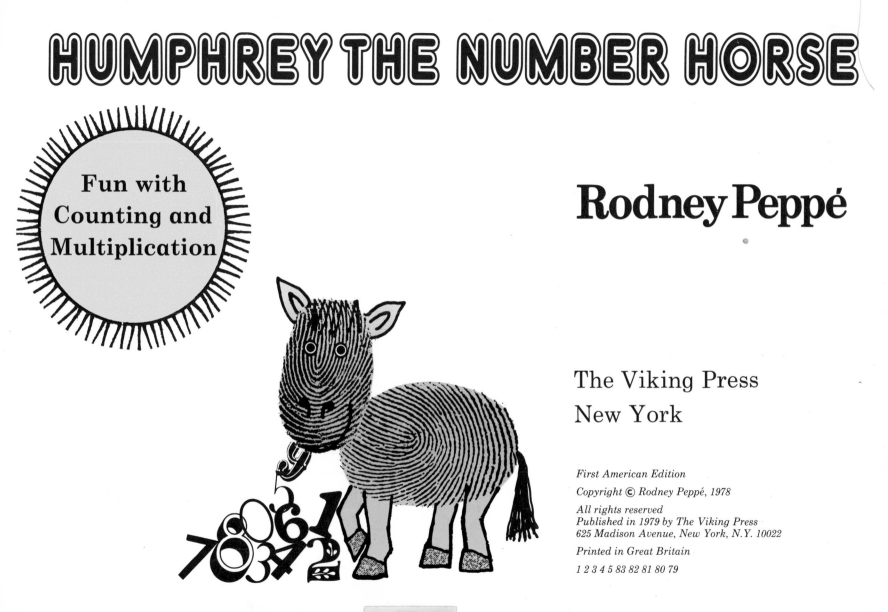

The Viking Press
New York

First American Edition

Copyright © Rodney Peppé, 1978

All rights reserved
Published in 1979 by The Viking Press
625 Madison Avenue, New York, N.Y. 10022

Printed in Great Britain

1 2 3 4 5 83 82 81 80 79

Humphrey the horse counted himself.
1 horse.
Humphrey said, "NEIGH!"

$1 \times 1 = 1$

How many horses can you count?
"Just one, of course," said Humphrey the horse.

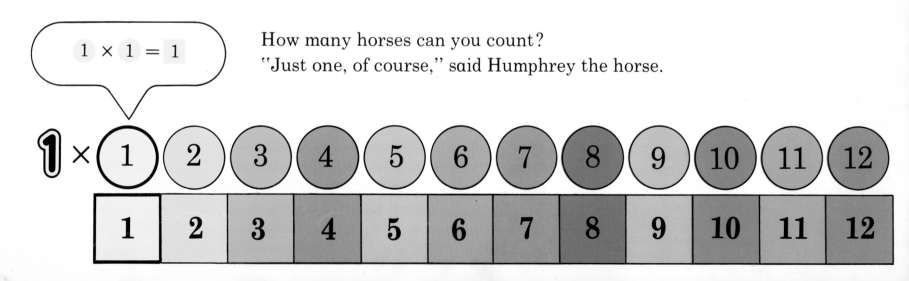

Humphrey the horse counted himself.
Then up wandered 2 cows.
The 2 cows said, "MOO, MOO!"
And they brought some friends . . .

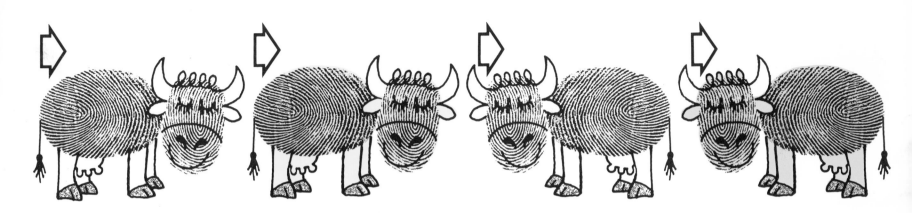

2 × 2 = 4

How many cows can you count?
2 groups of 2 cows is 4 cows.

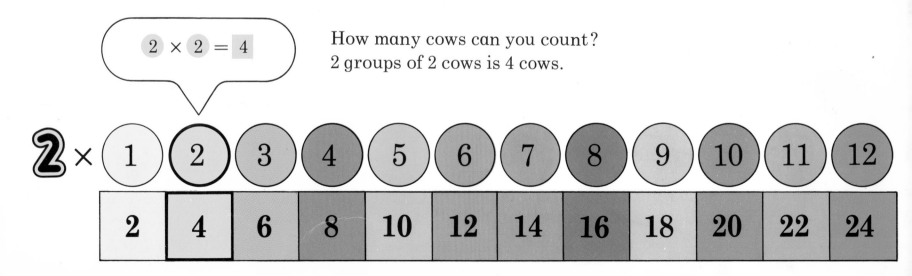

Humphrey the horse counted himself
and 2 cows.
Then up trotted 3 pigs.
The 3 pigs said, "OINK, OINK, OINK!"
And they brought some friends . . .

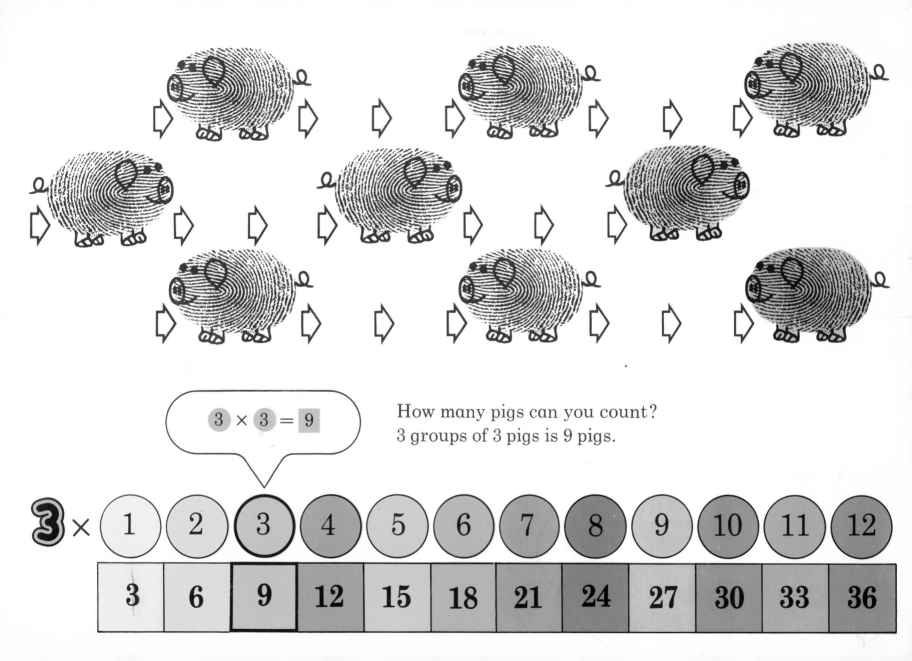

$3 \times 3 = 9$

How many pigs can you count?
3 groups of 3 pigs is 9 pigs.

$3 \times$

1	2	3	4	5	6	7	8	9	10	11	12
3	6	9	12	15	18	21	24	27	30	33	36

Humphrey the horse counted himself,
2 cows and 3 pigs.
Then up ran 4 sheep.
The 4 sheep said, "BAA, BAA, BAA, BAA!"
And they brought some friends . . .

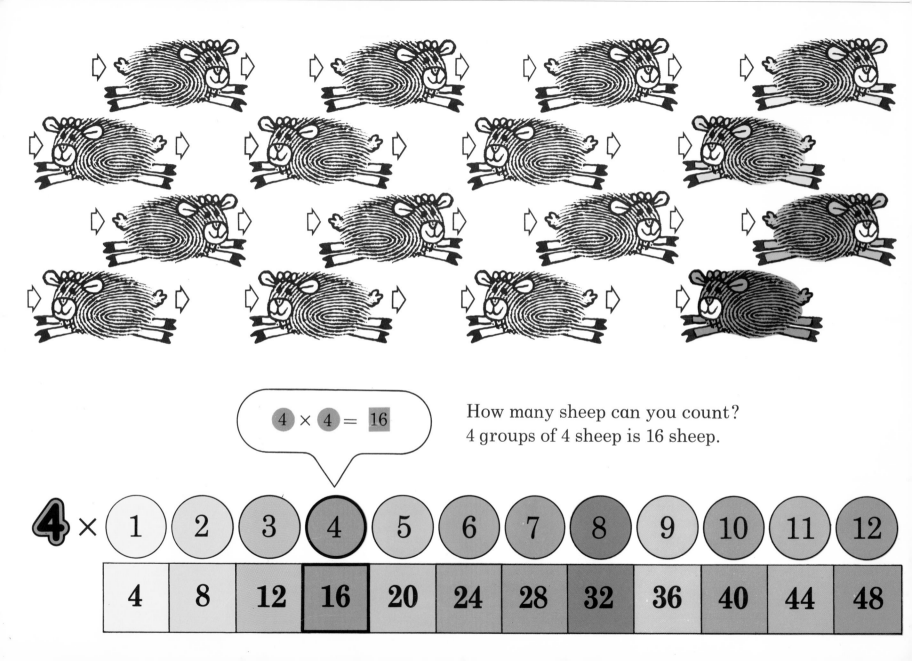

$4 \times 4 = 16$

How many sheep can you count?
4 groups of 4 sheep is 16 sheep.

$4 \times$

1	2	3	4	5	6	7	8	9	10	11	12
4	8	12	16	20	24	28	32	36	40	44	48

Humphrey the horse counted himself,
2 cows, 3 pigs and 4 sheep.
Then up bounded 5 dogs.
The five dogs said, "WUFF, WUFF, WUFF, WUFF, WUFF!"
And they brought some friends . . .

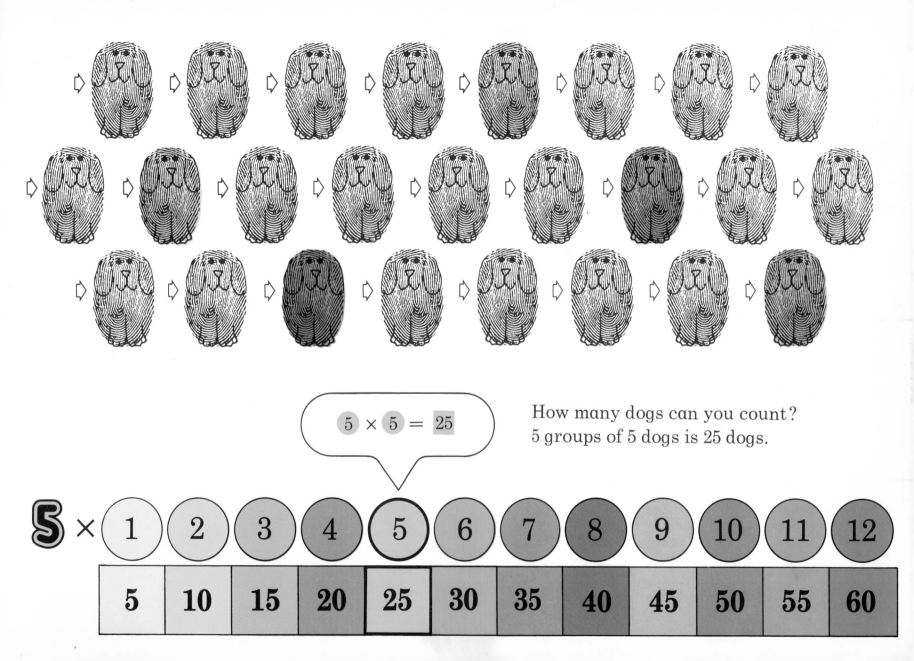

5 × 5 = 25

How many dogs can you count?
5 groups of 5 dogs is 25 dogs.

5 ×	1	2	3	4	5	6	7	8	9	10	11	12
	5	10	15	20	25	30	35	40	45	50	55	60

Humphrey the horse counted himself,
2 cows, 3 pigs, 4 sheep and 5 dogs.
Then up strolled 6 cats.
The 6 cats said, "MEOW, MEOW, MEOW, MEOW, MEOW, MEOW!"
And they brought some friends . . .

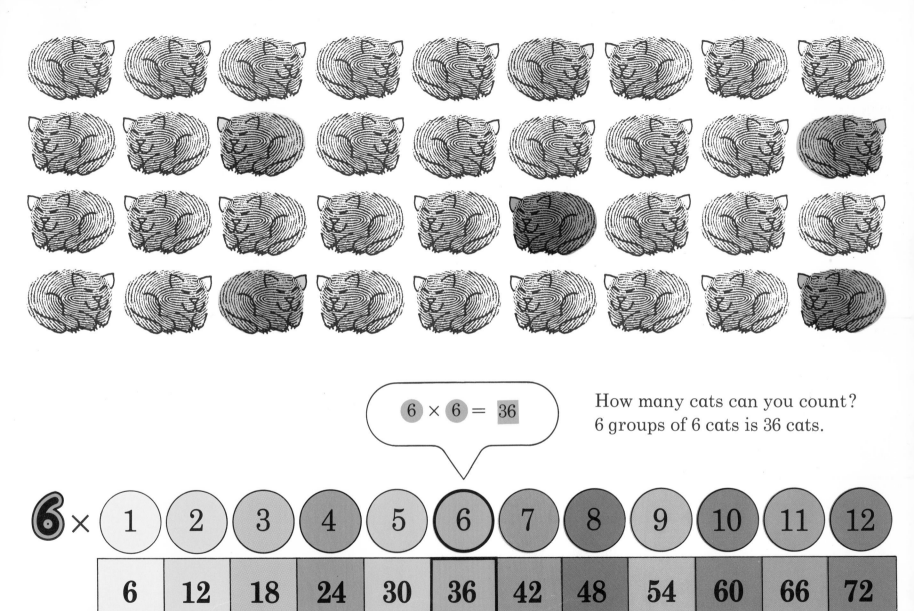

$6 \times 6 = 36$

How many cats can you count?
6 groups of 6 cats is 36 cats.

6 ×	1	2	3	4	5	6	7	8	9	10	11	12
	6	12	18	24	30	36	42	48	54	60	66	72

7

Humphrey the horse counted himself,
2 cows, 3 pigs, 4 sheep, 5 dogs and 6 cats.
Then in flew 7 owls.
The 7 owls said, "WHOO, WHOO, WHOO, WHOO, WHOO, WHOO, WHOO!"
And they brought some friends . . .

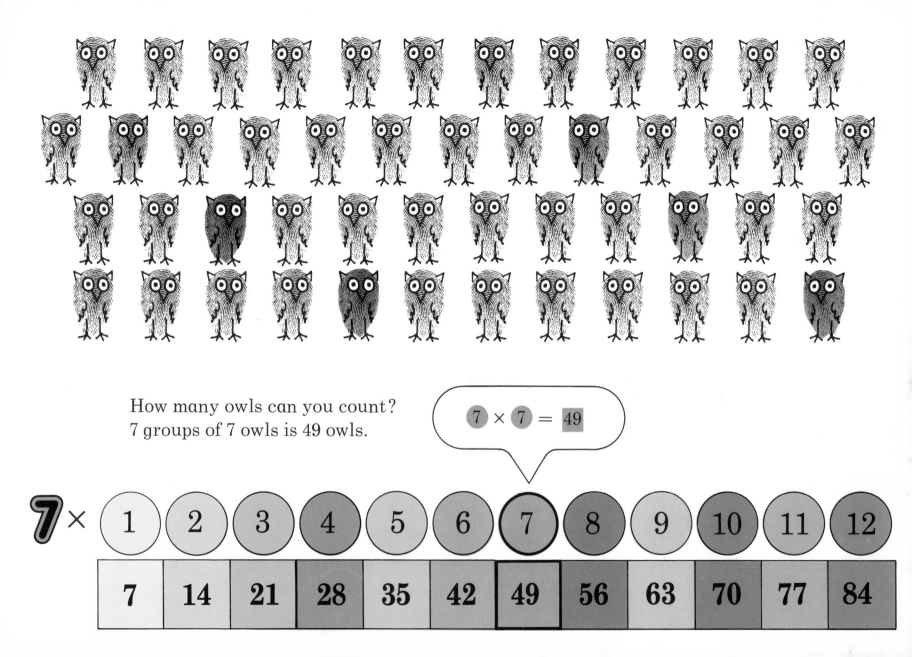

How many owls can you count?
7 groups of 7 owls is 49 owls.

7 × 7 = 49

7 ×

1	2	3	4	5	6	7	8	9	10	11	12
7	14	21	28	35	42	49	56	63	70	77	84

Humphrey the horse counted himself,
2 cows, 3 pigs, 4 sheep, 5 dogs, 6 cats and 7 owls.
Then up strutted 8 hens.
The eight hens said, "CLUCK, CLUCK, CLUCK, CLUCK, CLUCK, CLUCK,
CLUCK, CLUCK!"
And they brought some friends . . .

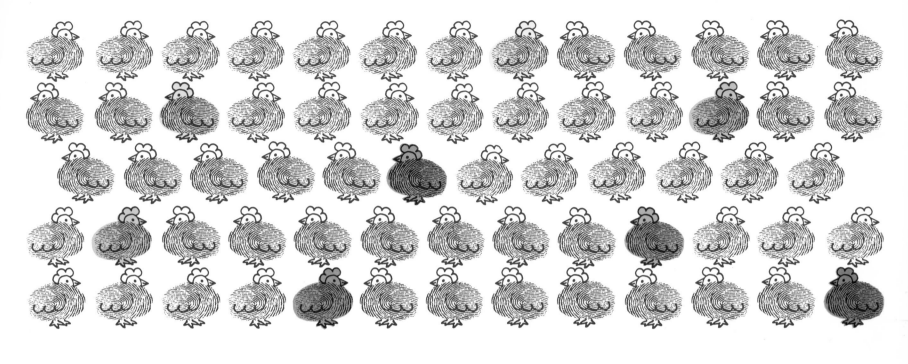

How many hens can you count?
8 groups of 8 hens is 64 hens.

$8 \times 8 = 64$

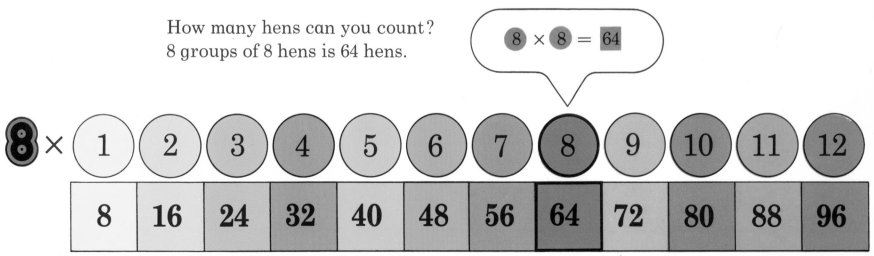

| 8 | 16 | 24 | 32 | 40 | 48 | 56 | 64 | 72 | 80 | 88 | 96 |

Humphrey the horse counted himself,
2 cows, 3 pigs, 4 sheep, 5 dogs, 6 cats, 7 owls and 8 hens.
Then up waddled 9 ducks.
The 9 ducks said, "QUACK, QUACK, QUACK, QUACK, QUACK, QUACK, QUACK, QUACK, QUACK!"
And they brought some friends . . .

How many ducks can you count?
9 groups of 9 ducks is 81 ducks.

$9 \times 9 = 81$

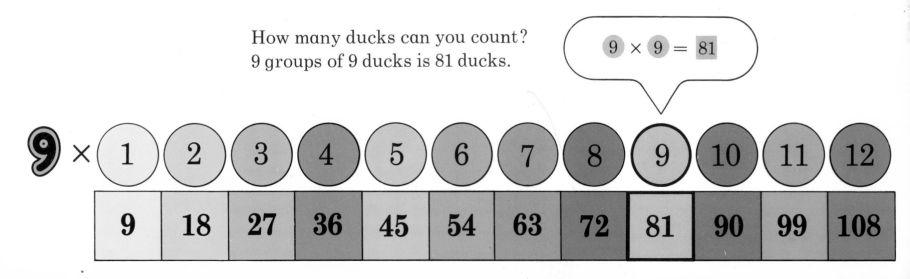

$9 \times$

1	2	3	4	5	6	7	8	9	10	11	12
9	18	27	36	45	54	63	72	81	90	99	108

10

Humphrey the horse counted himself,
2 cows, 3 pigs, 4 sheep, 5 dogs, 6 cats, 7 owls, 8 hens and 9 ducks.
Then up hopped 10 chicks.
The 10 chicks said, "CHEEP, CHEEP, CHEEP, CHEEP, CHEEP, CHEEP, CHEEP, CHEEP, CHEEP, CHEEP!"
And they brought some friends . . .

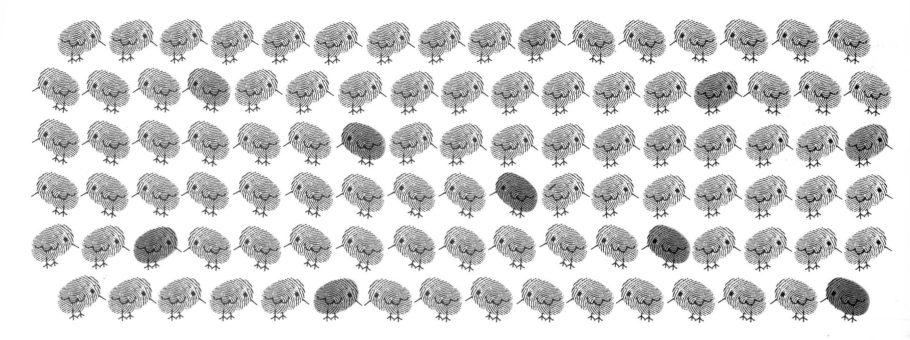

How many chicks can you count?
10 groups of 10 chicks is 100 chicks.

$10 \times 10 = 100$

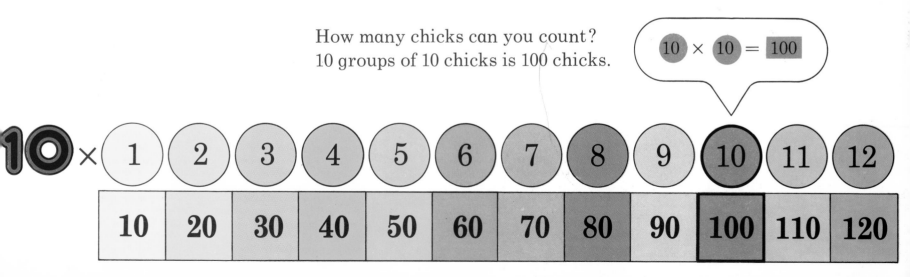

$10 \times$

1	2	3	4	5	6	7	8	9	10	11	12
10	20	30	40	50	60	70	80	90	100	110	120

11

Humphrey the horse counted himself,
2 cows, 3 pigs, 4 sheep, 5 dogs, 6 cats, 7 owls, 8 hens, 9 ducks and 10 chicks.
Then up jumped 11 frogs.
The 11 frogs said, "CROAK, CROAK, CROAK, CROAK, CROAK, CROAK, CROAK, CROAK, CROAK, CROAK, CROAK!"
And they brought some friends . . .

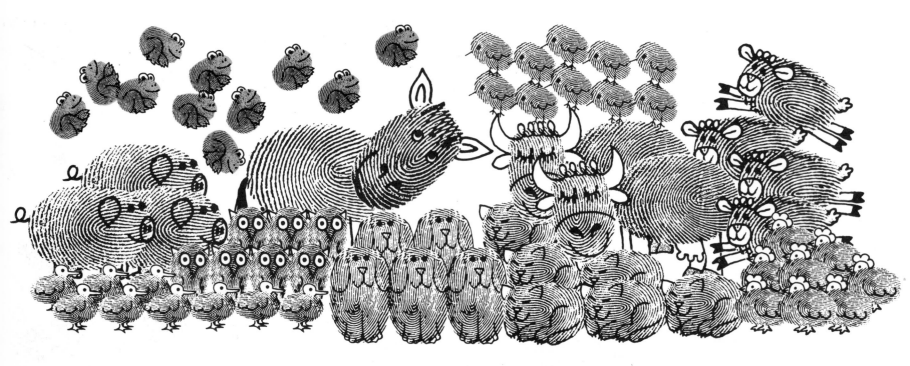

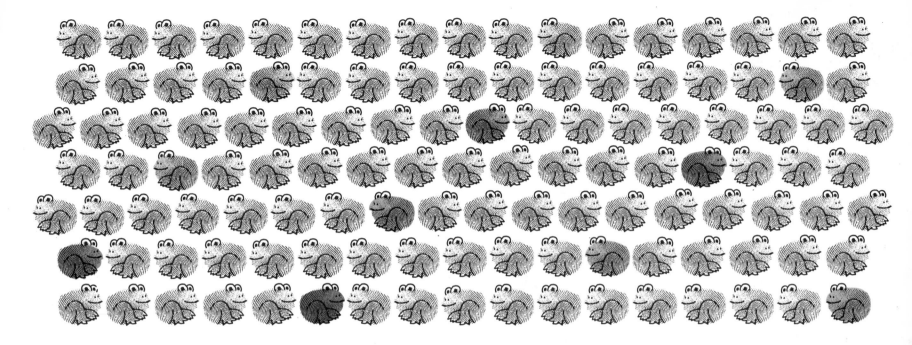

How many frogs can you count?
11 groups of 11 frogs is 121 frogs.

11 × 11 = 121

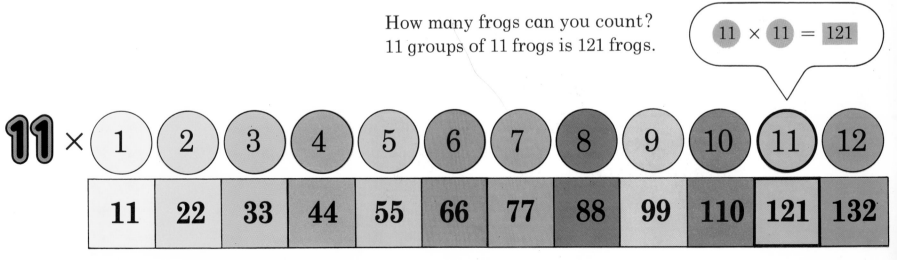

| 11 | 22 | 33 | 44 | 55 | 66 | 77 | 88 | 99 | 110 | 121 | 132 |

12

Humphrey the horse counted himself,
2 cows, 3 pigs, 4 sheep, 5 dogs, 6 cats, 7 owls, 8 hens, 9 ducks, 10 chicks and 11 frogs.
Then up scurried 12 mice.
The 12 mice said, "EEK, EEK, EEK, EEK, EEK, EEK, EEK, EEK, EEK, EEK, EEK, EEK!"
And they brought some friends . . .

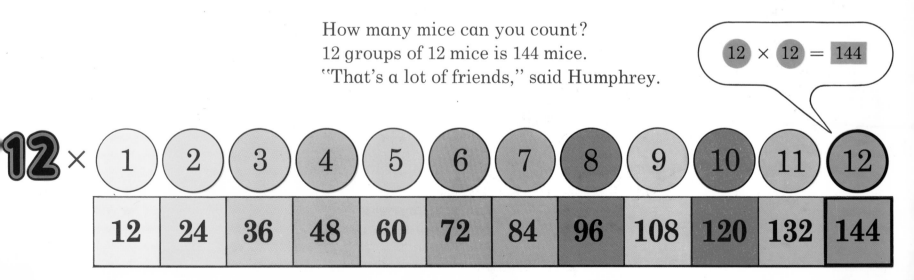

How many mice can you count?
12 groups of 12 mice is 144 mice.
"That's a lot of friends," said Humphrey.

12 × 12 = 144

12 × 1 2 3 4 5 6 7 8 9 10 11 12

| 12 | 24 | 36 | 48 | 60 | 72 | 84 | 96 | 108 | 120 | 132 | 144 |